Honk!

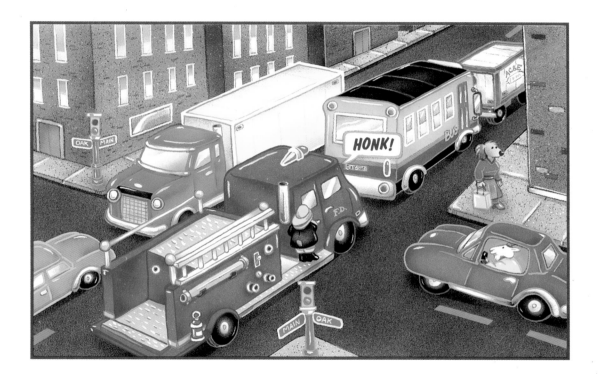

Written by Sue Smith
Illustrated by Linda Howard

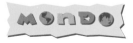

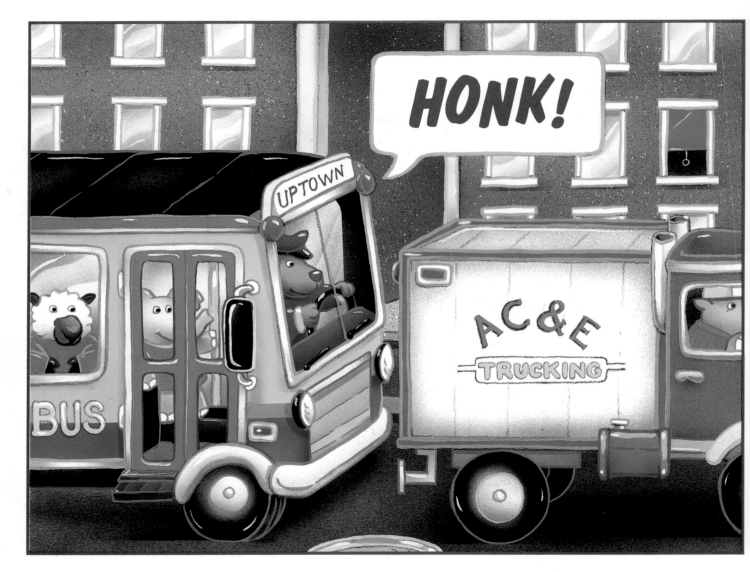

The bus honks at the truck.

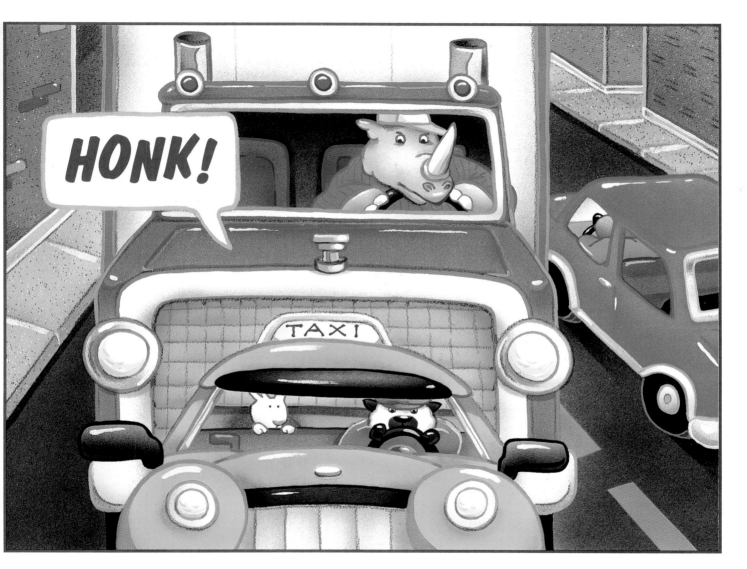

The truck honks at the taxi.

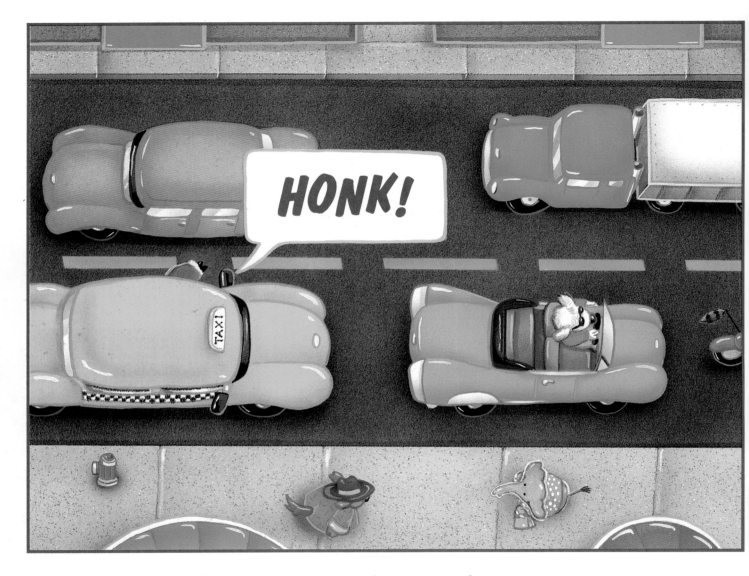

The taxi honks at the car.

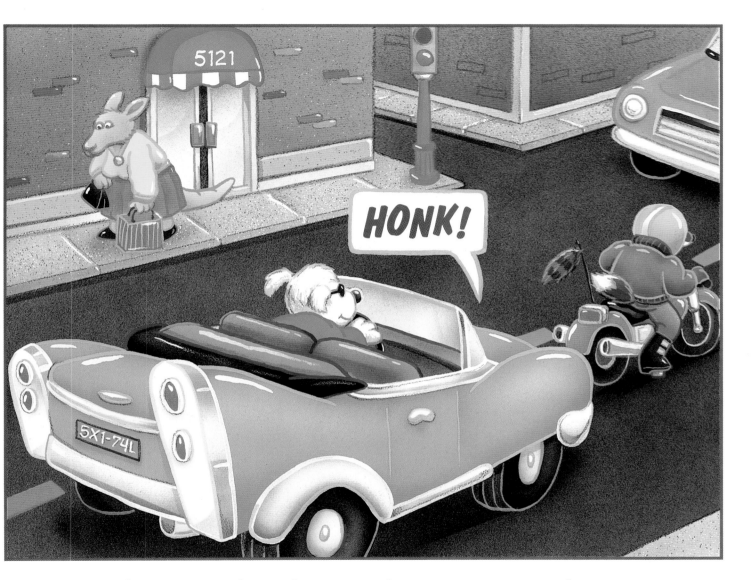

The car honks at the motorcycle.

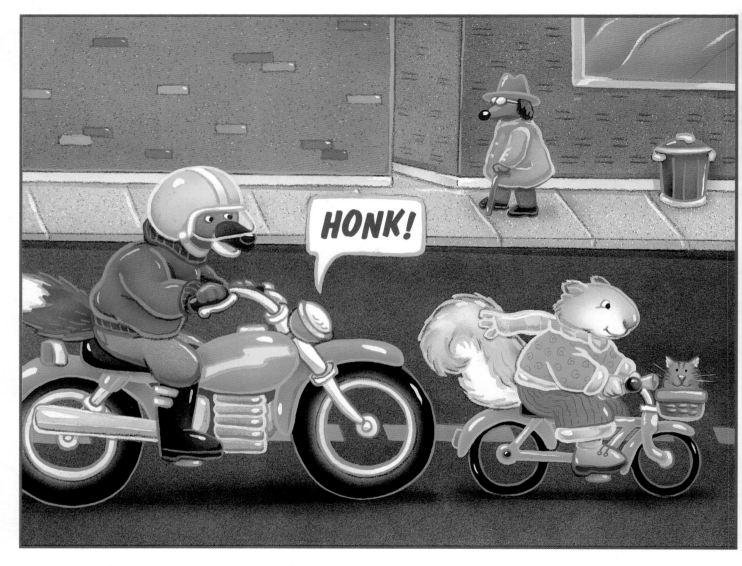

The motorcycle honks at the bicycle.

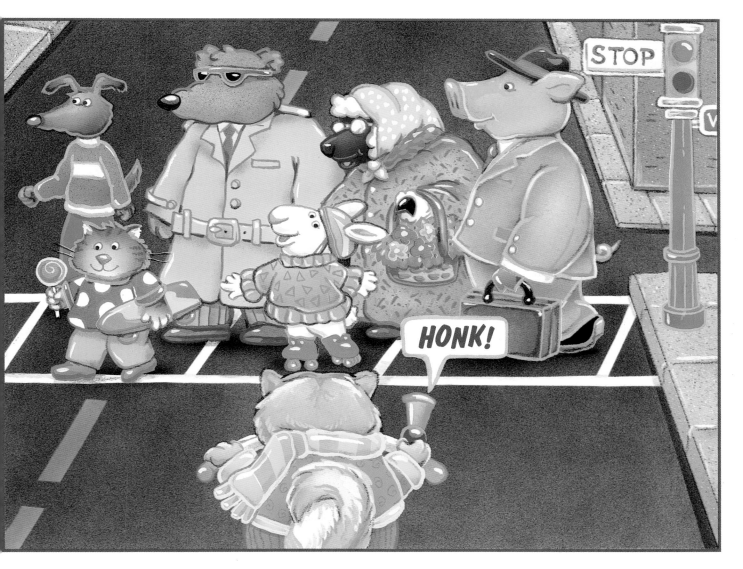

The bicycle honks at the crowd.

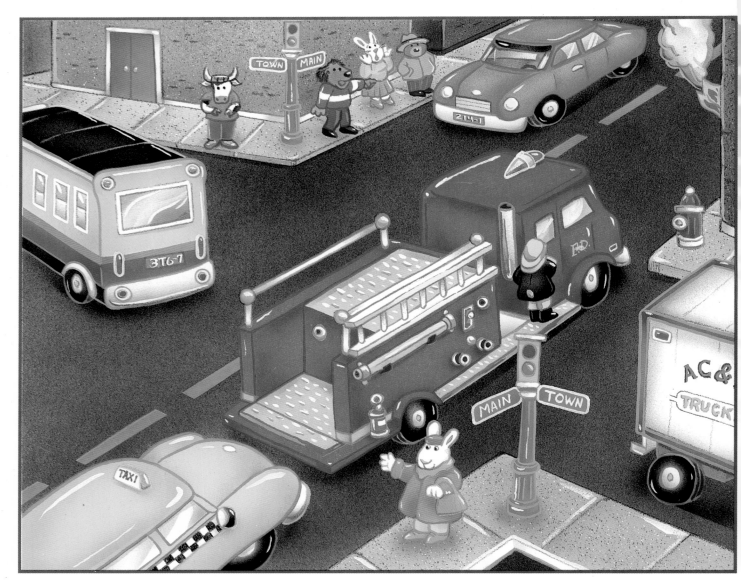